Two So Small

Two So Small

by Hazel Hutchins

art by Ruth Ohi

Annick Press Ltd. • Toronto • New York • Vancouver

© 2000 Hazel Hutchins (text)
© 2000 Ruth Ohi (illustrations)
Design by Sheryl Shapiro

Annick Press Ltd.

We acknowledge the support of the Canada Council for the Arts, the Ontario Arts Council, and the Government of Canada through the Book Publishing Industry Development Program (BPIDP) for our publishing activities.

Cataloguing in Publication Data

Hutchins, H.J. (Hazel J.)
        Two so small

ISBN 1-55037-651-9 (bound) ISBN 1-55037-650-0 (pbk.)

I. Ohi, Ruth. II. Title.

PS8565.U826T86 2000   jC813'.54   C00-930337-5
PZ7.H87Tw 2000

The art in this book was rendered in watercolor.
The text was typeset in Times Roman and Exquisit.

Distributed in Canada by: Published in the U.S.A. by Annick Press (U.S.) Ltd.
Firefly Books Ltd.   Distributed in the U.S.A. by:
3680 Victoria Park Avenue   Firefly Books (U.S.) Inc.
Willowdale, ON   P.O. Box 1338
M2H 3K1   Ellicott Station
                                   Buffalo, NY 14205

Manufactured in China.

visit us at: **www.annickpress.com**

To the imaginative students of Medicine Hat and their
merry band of Teacher Librarians. Thanks Grace.
—H.H.

A long time ago,

when the world was very different from,

and very much the same as, the way it is now,

a boy set out to visit his grandmother.

"Here is Grandmother's quilt, freshly washed," said his mother.

"Remember the way, for it is dangerous to go beyond our little land," said his father. "Under the bridge, around the trees, left at the big rock, in front of the waterfall and over the hill to Grandmother's house."

The boy hitched his goat to the cart and off they went.

They came to the bridge.

"Under or over?" asked the boy.

The goat didn't answer. She was nibbling sweet grass. Beside her was something long and round like a rope. The boy looked it up, down and all around.

"That is not a rope," he said.

He put the thing that was not a rope into the cart, and then—because on such a beautiful day he would surely make the right choice—off they went over the bridge.

They came to some trees.

"Through or around?" asked the boy.

The goat didn't answer. She was eating wildflowers. Beside her was something round and shiny like a dinner plate. The boy looked it up, down and all around.

"That is not a dinner plate," he said.

He put the thing that was not a dinner plate into the cart. Off they went through the trees.

The trees grew taller. Had they lost their way?
But at last they came to a big rock.
"Left or right?" asked the boy.
The goat didn't answer. She was munching
tender moss. Beside her was something pointed

and colorful like a tent. The boy looked it up,
down and all around.

"That is not a tent," he said.

He folded the thing that was not a tent into the
cart. Off they went, turning right at the big rock.

At the waterfall, they rested.

"In front or behind?" asked the boy.

The goat didn't answer. She was drinking from a quiet pool. Lying in the pool was something squishy and lumpy like a jellyfish. The boy looked it up, down and all around.

"That is not a jellyfish," he said.

He hung the thing that was not a jellyfish from the back of the cart.

"Baaaaa!" said the goat.

"The hill!" cried the boy.

Off they went behind the waterfall and over the hill, and there on the other side was . . .

. . . a great big baby. It was a baby giant—a very sad, very big baby giant with one shoe half off, a mixed-up shirt, a sunburned nose and an empty baby bottle.

The boy was afraid. Humans and giants are always afraid of each other. Giants are so much larger. Humans are so much sneakier. But the baby looked so sad and so lost that the boy simply could not run away.

"Don't cry, baby," called the boy. "My goat and I will help you."

From the cart, the boy took the rope that was not a rope. The goat and the boy tugged and pulled. Soon the baby's shoe was back on its foot and tied with a double knot.

"Shlace," said the baby, which is baby-giant talk for *shoelace*.

The boy took the dinner plate that was not a dinner plate. He unhooked his belt. The goat and the boy tugged and pulled. Soon the baby's shirt was neatly fastened.

"Bunt!" said the baby, which is baby-giant talk for *button*.

The boy took the tent that was not a tent. The goat and the boy tugged and pulled. Soon the baby's head was protected from the sun.

"At!" said the baby, which is baby-giant talk for *hat*.

The boy took the jellyfish that was not a jelly-fish. With the help of the goat he filled the bottle. Well, there was only enough to fill it partway, but the milk was especially delicious because of the sweet grass, wildflowers and tender moss the goat had eaten. They tugged and pulled and handed the baby its bottle, topped with the lost nipple.

The boy went and brought
Grandmother's freshly washed quilt.
"Blankie," said the baby.
With the sun setting behind a
mountain, the goat, the boy and the
baby curled up and fell asleep.

While they were sleeping, the mountain that was not a mountain found the baby.

Her heart was filled with joy, for giants love their babies every bit as much as humans do. Then she was afraid and angry to see a boy and a goat! Finally she saw the shoelace with its double knot, the button with its new thread, the hat set gently, the last drop of sweet milk and the tiny quilt.

"All done by two so small," she smiled, and gathered them up in her hand.

They awoke with alarm. So gently were they held, however, that they soon realized the giant meant no harm. As she lifted them back into the land of humans, they were even able to see what lay below.

Which is why, as they were set down, they knew exactly what to do. They went under the bridge, around the trees, left at the big rock, in front of the waterfall and over the hill to arrive at Grandmother's house . . .

just in time for supper.